REBELS

102900 862118 000012 GHOST SHIP 001036 10

Rebel Faction

001000 IT 10

010

ART ATTACK

**Based on the episode "Art Attack,"
written by Greg Weisman**

Adapted by Brooke Vitale

© & TM 2014 Lucasfilm Ltd.

Published by Disney • Lucasfilm Press, an imprint of Disney Book Group. No part of this book may be reproduced or transmitted in any form or by any means, electronic or mechanical, including photocopying, recording, or by any information storage and retrieval system, without written permission from the publisher. For information address Disney • Lucasfilm Press, 1101 Flower Street, Glendale, California 91201.

Printed in China

First Edition, December 2014
1 3 5 7 9 10 8 6 4 2

ISBN 978-1-4847-2608-2
T425-2382-5-14356

Visit the official *Star Wars* website at: www.starwars.com
This book was printed on paper created from a sustainable source.

LUCASFILM
PRESS

Los Angeles • New York

It was a quiet night. The stars twinkled in the sky. On the ground, stormtroopers patrolled the area.

"Move along! This is a restricted area," a stormtrooper told a passing civilian. The stormtrooper shoved the civilian to the ground and kept walking.

From a wall high above, Sabine watched the scene unfold. Suddenly, Hera's voice came over the radio.

"This is *Ghost*. We're in position and awaiting your diversion."

"Copy that," Sabine said. "This is going to be fun."

Sabine peered at the world below her.
She was standing over an Imperial airfield.
TIE fighters surrounded her and spotlights
searched the perimeter.

Sabine ducked to avoid a roving light.
Then, taking a deep breath, she dropped
to the ground.

Sabine didn't have a moment to waste.
Peering around the side of a TIE fighter,
she checked that the coast was clear. Then
she took off across the field.

Elsewhere on the airfield, the two stormtroopers continued to patrol. Suddenly, one of them stopped walking. "You hear that?" he asked his partner.

"I don't hear—" the second stormtrooper started. Then he stopped and listened more closely. "Wait, yeah. What is that?" he asked.

Behind the stormtroopers, a soft spraying sound filled the air.

The first stormtrooper motioned across the airfield. "This way."

The stormtroopers quietly walked across the field, following the sound. As they passed between two TIE fighters, they stopped in their tracks.

"What in the—" the first stormtrooper started.

In front of them stood Sabine. She was spray-painting a huge purple starbird onto the wing of a fighter.

The stormtroopers raised their weapons, but Sabine just kept painting. Soon she had completed the starbird—except for the beak.

"W-Well, stand down!" the second stormtrooper ordered.

"Or we shoot!" the first stormtrooper added.

Sabine turned toward the stormtroopers. "Okay. Shoot."

Sabine ducked behind the cockpit of the TIE fighter just as the stormtroopers turned their weapons on her.

"You call that shooting?" Sabine called. "I think you boys need a little more time on the practice range."

The stormtroopers knew when they were outmatched. Speaking into his comlink, the first stormtrooper said, "This is TK-626. There's an intruder on site."

"On our way," a voice answered.

The stormtroopers turned in circles, looking for Sabine.

"Where did—" the first stormtrooper began.

Suddenly, Sabine jumped out and ran past them. "Over here, bucket-heads," she called.

"There!" the second stormtrooper cried.

The first stormtrooper spun around and fired at Sabine. He just missed, and she ducked behind another fighter.

"You guys are too predictable," Sabine taunted.

Sabine wove her way between TIE fighters until she was safely away from the stormtroopers. Then she called out, "Always by the book. I read your book."

Just then, the stormtroopers' commander appeared with three more stormtroopers.

"What do we got?" he asked.

"One intruder in Mando gear, still at large," the second stormtrooper answered.

Sabine watched from above as the stormtroopers came up with a plan to find her. Finally, the commander gave his stormtroopers their orders. "Split up," he said, pointing in two directions.

The stormtroopers dispersed and Sabine leaped down from her hiding spot. She couldn't stand the thought of leaving her art unfinished!

"There. Perfect!" Sabine said, painting the starbird's beak.

Suddenly, a stormtrooper appeared behind her. Sabine raised her arms in defeat . . .

. . . and kicked out her leg, sweeping the stormtrooper off his feet.

The stormtrooper fired at Sabine, but she was already gone.

"Ha! Too slow," she taunted.

Sabine raced from TIE fighter to TIE fighter, drawing the stormtroopers' attention.

"Intruder was headed your way!" the commander yelled into his comlink.

"I had her," a confused stormtrooper replied.

Just then, the stormtroopers noticed something. The TIE fighter in front of them had a purple starbird painted on it.

"Isn't this where we started?" the stormtrooper asked. "Uh-oh."

The stormtrooper leaned in, looking more closely at the starbird. It had a red eye. And the eye was blinking.

It was a bomb!

Sabine dropped to the ground and ran.

Suddenly . . . *BOOM!*

The TIE fighter exploded, knocking the stormtroopers over and turning them all purple.

"That was some diversion, Sabine," Hera said over the radio. "Did the job so well we can see the explosion from here."

Pulling off her helmet, Sabine turned to look at her work. The stormtroopers were just starting to get to their feet.

Sabine grinned. "Forget the explosion," she answered. "Look at the color!"

And then, putting her helmet back on, she calmly walked away to join Hera aboard the *Ghost*.